The Mouse and The Rodeo

By Nancy Mullen

PAGE PUBLISHING, INC.
New York, NY

First originally published by Page Publishing, Inc. 2015

ISBN 978-1-68213-151-0 (pbk)
ISBN 978-1-68213-152-7 (digital)

Printed in the United States of America

I

Easton was a little mouse that lived in a beautiful meadow with his mom and dad. He was an only child and spent most of his time playing in his room. The only time he was allowed outside was when both his parents were with him.

Easton was sheltered.

One night, after his mom gave him a bath and a bed-time snack, Easton was lying in bed. He thought what it would be like to join a rodeo. The night before his dad had read him a book about the rodeo and Easton was intrigued.

He thought about how much fun it would be to ride a horse, wear a big cowboy hat, and even better, to ride a bull!

Easton decided he was going to find a rodeo.

Easton fell asleep.

II

The next morning after breakfast, Easton found every book he could find about rodeos. He was so excited to start his journey that he never realized he had sat on his cat.

Every day when Easton came home from school, he would grab a snack, lay on his bed, and read. And read he did. He read and read and read.

Easton was tired.

When he decided he was finished reading, he ran down the hall screaming, "It's time! It's time! I'm ready to go to the rodeo!" But first he had to pick himself up off the floor. Easton fell over his cat.

Easton's dad had found a rodeo to take Easton to. So off they went. Easton was so excited he could hardly breath.

"Come on, Easton, let's go!" said his mom. So Easton kissed his cat good-bye and off they went.

Easton's cat was happy.

III

Easton fell asleep in the back seat. "Wake up, Easton!" said his dad "We're here!"

Easton jumped up and rubbed his eyes. He couldn't believe he was here. Easton had chills. Holding his mom's and dad's hand, they chose their seats and sat down.

Wearing a big cowboy hat and smiling real big, in fact so big his face disappeared, Easton felt right at home.

When the rodeo was over, Easton started screaming and screaming, "No! I don't want to leave!" So the
screaming continued.

Easton's face was red from all the screaming he was
doing that he never realized he dropped his popcorn and
his hat.

Easton was mad.

IV

The popcorn and hat landed on a little bull, which by the way didn't seem to bother the bull at all. In fact, he wore the hat while eating Easton's popcorn. Easton finally stopped screaming when he realized he dropped his popcorn and his hat, which sat perfectly on the little bull.

Easton hollered over the rail. "Hey! That's my hat and popcorn! What do you think you are doing?" The little bull answered without even looking up, "Well, sir, I'm eating popcorn and wearing a cowboy hat. What are you doing?"

Easton wasn't happy and without thinking he jumped over the rail. The only problem was Easton had jumped too far and landed in a big bowl of cotton candy!

V

Easton heard his mom and dad calling him. "I'm down here!" he screamed still lying in the bowl of cotton candy.

"What are you doing down there?" his mom said.

"Don't ask!" said Easton, who was now climbing out.

"Stay there," said his dad.

But Easton was on the move. By the time his parents reached Easton, the little bull had finished the popcorn and was looking for something to drink.

"Let's go!" said Easton's dad.

But Easton said, "No, no! No! No!"

Well, this went on for ten minutes until his dad picked him up and said, "We are going!"

Easton was really mad.

VI

The little bull, now stuffed, got up and followed them. Neither Easton, nor his parents realized they were being followed because Easton started to scream again.

Easton screamed all the way home. Easton finally stopped screaming only because he fell asleep.

The next morning, he got up and ran down the hall. Tripping over his cat, he rolled into the kitchen where his mom was making breakfast.

"Good morning Easton," said his mom. "Are you feeling better?"

Easton went to answer but all he could do was squeak! "Squeak, squeak, squeak!"

"Well," said his mom "You were screaming so much you lost your voice. Are you happy now?"

He quietly ate his breakfast and went back into his room.

Every time he opened his mouth a squeak came out.

VII

Easton now has the hiccups. With every hiccup, he would squeak. He was hiccupping and squeaking so much, he bounced off his bed and was lying on the floor.

He heard laughing. With every hiccup and squeak the laughter got louder. Then he heard "Hi!" He looked under his bed, and there he saw the little bull.

"You sound funny," said the bull.

Easton just lay on the floor staring at the bull. The little bull said, "You were so busy screaming you never saw me following you."

Easton tried to speak. "Squeak."

The little bull continued, "I sat on the bumper of your car all the way home, and well, here I am. I see your hiccups have stopped."

Easton sat up, squeaking, but was happy no more hiccups.

The little bull continued, "I snuck in your bedroom, and well, here I am."

Easton started laughing and squeaking. He found a crayon and a piece of paper and wrote, "Do you want some popcorn?"

"Yes!" said the little bull. "Yes. But first here is your hat."

Easton smiled.

About the Author:

Nancy Mullen was born and raised in Central New Jersey.
She is married with one daughter and six grandchildren.
She now resides in Oro Valley, Arizona.

CPSIA information can be obtained
at www.ICGtesting.com
Printed in the USA
BVHW092150041120
592527BV00003B/33